Hello Kitty
and friends

The TV Star

·A HELLO KITTY ADVENTURE·

Hello Kitty

and friends

The TV Star

·A HELLO KITTY ADVENTURE·

HarperCollins *Children's Books*

MEET Hello Kitty
and friends

Hello Kitty

Mimmy

Tammy

Mama

Papa

Grandpa

Grandma

Fifi

Dear Daniel

With special thanks to
Linda Chapman and Michelle Misra

First published in Great Britain by HarperCollins *Children's Books* in 2014

www.harpercollins.co.uk
1 3 5 7 9 10 8 6 4 2
ISBN: 978-000-751588-2

Printed and bound in England by Clays Ltd, St Ives plc.

Conditions of Sale

MIX
Paper from
responsible sources
www.fsc.org **FSC® C007454**

FSC™ is a non-profit international organisation established to promote
the responsible management of the world's forests. Products carrying the
FSC label are independently certified to assure consumers that they come
from forests that are managed to meet the social, economic and
ecological needs of present and future generations,
and other controlled sources.

Find out more about HarperCollins and the environment at
www.harpercollins.co.uk/green

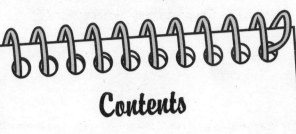

Contents

Fifi's News!

Hello Kitty sat at the top of the slide. She covered her eyes with both hands before sliding all the way down to the bottom, laughing and calling as she went. **Wheeeeeeee!** It was a sunny day and Hello Kitty couldn't think of anywhere she would rather be than in the

park with her friends. Dear Daniel followed

on behind and Tammy after that. They landed

with a bump at the bottom. Now all that they

needed was for Fifi to arrive at the

park and complete the group!

The four of them were really good friends and together they made up the Friendship Club. They met to do all sorts of *fun* things like baking and dancing and painting. They were going to a meeting at Fifi's house that afternoon, only it was too nice to be inside right now so they had decided to go to the park first instead.

Hello Kitty looked across the grass to where her mama was sitting in the shade of the trees with Hello Kitty's twin sister, Mimmy, who was playing her flute.

Just then, Fifi arrived and saw them. She looked very excited as she came running across the grass to join the rest of the Friendship Club.

She had a scrapbook
under one arm and
was waving a
piece of paper in
the other. Hello
Kitty called to Dear
Daniel and Tammy to
come over quickly, and they
ran with her to meet Fifi. She DID look very
excited – what could she **possibly** have
to tell them?

Fifi jumped up and down. She had just found
out that she was going to be a TV presenter for
a day!

How super! Everyone gasped, Hello Kitty high-fived her and Dear Daniel and Tammy cheered – it was **brilliant!** Everyone wanted to ask Fifi questions so she got them all to slow down so that she could answer them one at a time.

Dear Daniel wanted to know what the show was going to be about, so Fifi told him that it was for *Fun and Friendship* – a programme about family and friends.

Tammy wanted to know **what** Fifi had had to do to become a presenter.

So Fifi talked all about how she had made a friendship scrapbook. She had just been putting it together for fun, but her mother had seen it and sent it into the programme. They had liked it so much they had asked her to go on to the show!

Hello Kitty *and friends*

Hello Kitty asked what was in the scrapbook.
Fifi told her that the first page was all about
friendship and who her friends were, but then
after that there were lots of different pages:

Special family moments

Travel with friends

Birthdays

Recipes

There were lots of glittery drawings and photos in it, and stickers too. It was beautiful!

They all started chattering at once, wondering what Fifi would have to do when she was presenting the programme. Fifi declared excitedly that she would be presenting a short section where she would show the viewers how to make a friendship scrapbook of their own. It sounded like really good fun! **Hooray!**

Mama poured everyone a fizzy pink lemonade while they talked and talked, turning over the pages of Fifi's scrapbook.

It had a purple cover and was decorated all over with little silver stars. Hello Kitty liked the birthdays' page *best*.

Fifi had stuck in photos of them all and labelled them with their names, their dates of birth and some old birthday cards. Dear Daniel liked the page on travel where Fifi had put tickets from the different trips they had been on together. There was even an old

concert ticket from when

they had all gone to see

the band the Fizzy Pops.

Tammy liked the recipe for

chocolate friendship muffins best. **Yummy!**

HK TICKETS — HK TICKETS

Fizzy Pops!
3RD JULY
Concert in the park

But the scrapbook wasn't quite finished,

whispered Fifi – she wanted to put in more

photos and make some more pages before

she went on the show to

talk about it, but she

was running out of

time! Filming for the

programme was on

Monday – just after the weekend. There wasn't long to put it all together...

Hello Kitty grinned. She knew exactly who could help – the Friendship Club, of course! They could start that very afternoon.

Fifi grinned gratefully. The Friendship Club was the best!

A Bit of a Wobble

The Friendship Club played happily in the

park for the next half an hour. Just as they

were about to leave to go to Fifi's house, an

ice-cream van appeared at the park gates, and

Mama offered to buy them all ice creams! What

would they all have? Hello Kitty just couldn't decide whether to have a chocolate delight or a strawberry surprise. Everyone ordered their treats and Hello Kitty **finally** settled on a double-chocolate ice cream before they headed back out through the park and down the tree-lined streets. They passed a line of shops, and eventually they reached Fifi's house.

Fifi's mother opened the door and let them in. Mama White and Mimmy had to go to Mimmy's flute practice, so they waved goodbye and hurried off. Hello Kitty was surprised at how busy Fifi's house was! There were three painters and decorators there, all very busy painting the walls and ceilings. The Friendship Club had to climb over dust sheets and pots of paints to get to Fifi's playroom. Once they sat down, Fifi produced a whole box of crafting materials:

Glue

Scissors

Coloured papers

Stars

Glitter

They all sat down at the table and got cutting and sticking for the friendship scrapbook. It was a whole lot of **fun!**

Hello Kitty started to draw little glittery

hearts around the names on the birthday page,

and Tammy suggested she should do them in

purple to match the cover. Then Tammy drew

lines to link the photos on Fifi's family page to

make a family tree. It looked totally super!

As they worked, they questioned Fifi about every detail of the TV show. How long would she be on TV for? What would she have to say? What would happen if she forgot her lines or something went wrong?

Fifi got quieter and quieter, and started to look a bit anxious. She hadn't really *thought* about things like that.

The room was a hive of activity as they carried on sticking and pasting, and everyone was concentrating hard on the pages they were

working on. After a while, Hello Kitty looked
over her shoulder and saw Fifi slipping out of
the room, still looking a bit worried. Where was
she going? Fifi mumbled **something** about
getting more photos. Then she disappeared.

Hello Kitty looked thoughtful, then put down
the page she was working on and followed her.

It wasn't like Fifi to look so anxious. Whatever could be the matter? Hello Kitty looked around. Fifi wasn't in the hallway, so she must be upstairs; Hello Kitty made her way up to the next floor, where the bedrooms were. She walked down the landing and pushed the door to Fifi's room open. Fifi was sitting on the bed. She was facing the window, but didn't seem to be looking at **anything**. Hello Kitty hurried over. Was Fifi OK?

Fifi looked up, took a deep breath and shook her head. Hello Kitty hugged her as Fifi told her what the problem was. She loved the idea of being a presenter and appearing on a TV show,

but she realised she hadn't really thought about

everything that could go wrong. What if she

forgot her lines? What if she did mess it all up?

What if she got everything *wrong?*

Hello Kitty was surprised. She reminded Fifi of all the ice-skating competitions she had been in – she hadn't been scared doing those!

But Fifi explained that somehow ice-skating was different – she'd been doing it for a long time, and when she was on the ice everything else just slipped away. It wouldn't be like that on TV – she was going to be talking, and acting in front of the cameras!

Everyone would be watching!

Hello Kitty hugged her tightly and asserted that Fifi would be just fine. And suddenly, she had an idea! Why didn't they have a practice run where Fifi could do her talk for the Friendship Club – just like a dress rehearsal for a play. If she could do her talk in front of her friends, doing it in front of the camera would be **easy!**

Fifi still looked unsure, and breathed that maybe Hello Kitty would be better at this than her. Perhaps she should get her mother to phone up the show and see if Hello Kitty could do it instead?

Hello Kitty declared loudly that she shouldn't be silly. Fifi was going to do the talk *perfectly* – there wasn't anything to worry about! She just needed to get her scrapbook completely ready and have a proper practice. To get her started, Hello Kitty reminded Fifi that she had come up here to get some more photos.

Oh yes! Fifi dived under her bed

and pulled out a box. The box was a beautiful **glittery** gold and had pretty pearls stuck on it. Fifi whispered that she always hid anything secret like the box, under her bed, when she didn't want

her little brother or sister to find it. They never thought to look there! Hello Kitty giggled.

Fifi pulled out some photos and laid them out on the floor. Hello Kitty held up a photo of Fifi as a baby in her parent's arms, with her tongue stuck out, and giggled some more. Fifi looked over and laughed. She did look rather funny in that one. And what about this one – Fifi in her first nativity play. She was dressed up as a sheep! They could all go on the special family moment's page. Soon the two friends were both laughing and giggling, and Fifi looked much happier. Perhaps everything would be OK after all!

Hello Kitty and Fifi eventually put the photos

away and went back downstairs. Tammy and

Dear Daniel looked up; where had they been,

they wanted to know? Fifi took a deep breath

and explained that she had been feeling a bit

nervous about the show, but that Hello Kitty

had made her feel **much** better! They

were going to have a dress rehearsal tomorrow

where Fifi could practise in front of them all.

Tammy and Dear Daniel smiled; that was a

great idea.

Not only that, but Hello Kitty had just thought of something even better! Maybe they should do something to take Fifi's mind off the TV show over the weekend... a trip to Waterworld – the water park not too far away! That would be just the thing! As everyone squealed and nodded Hello Kitty clapped her hands. She would ask Mama today if they could go on Saturday!

Everyone **smiled** at each other and agreed. A trip to Waterworld was just what they needed!

Practice Run

At school the next day, everyone was just as
excited about the TV show as the Friendship
Club had been. They crowded around Fifi,
asking her lots of questions and looking at the
scrapbook. Hello Kitty glanced worriedly at her

friend from behind the crowd. What if all these questions made Fifi feel nervous again? But luckily, Fifi seemed to be all right.

Their form teacher Miss Davey clapped her hands and asked everyone to sit down at their desks. They had **a lot** to get through!

For the rest of the day, the class worked hard at their story-writing and maths, and on their art projects. The bell finally rang at the end of the day, and as they came out of the classroom and into the bright sunshine Fifi chatted happily. Mama was there to pick them all up and take them back to Hello Kitty's house for the big dress rehearsal.

As soon as they arrived, the friends got down to work cutting and pasting. When the scrapbook was finally ready, Fifi cleared the table and laid out *everything* she needed to explain how to make a friendship scrapbook, just like she would on TV. Tammy, Hello Kitty and Dear Daniel sat on the floor in front of her and waited patiently.

It was time for Fifi to begin her talk! First, she spoke about family and friendship and the special people she had put into her scrapbook. There was her family – her mama, papa and naughty little brother and sister. And there was everyone in the Friendship Club of course!

Fifi had to try not to smile as she said Hello

Kitty, Fifi and Dear Daniel's names. She tried

to pretend she was doing the talk for real and

talked about each of her friends, explaining why

they were so **special.**

She started with Dear Daniel, saying how

much he loved sports, making models, and all

animals, even creepy crawlies! Then she went on about what a good listener Tammy was and how she made up the best stories and played fun tricks. When it was Hello Kitty's turn, Hello Kitty couldn't keep the *smile* off her face as Fifi praised her for being organised, stylish and the best friend ever.

Fifi showed them how to make a page with photos of each friend and a list of their special qualities underneath. Then she started to talk about the birthdays' page. Hello Kitty's was the first photo she held up with her birthday beside it – the 1st of November. Because it was the first day of the month it was **easy** to remember, but by having a friendship birthdays' page it made it hard to forget anyone's. Fifi cut out some old birthday cards and showed how she had pasted them into the book.

Then she showed them how to stick photos and stickers all around the different people and link them with lines to make a family and a friendship tree. When Fifi finally held it up for everyone to see it looked very pretty and *sparkly.*

She smiled. So that was how you made a friendship scrapbook!

Her friends gave her a round of applause and Fifi beamed.

See! Hello Kitty smiled and pointed out how easy it could be when you were on a roll – just like when Fifi was ice-skating – and that once you got into it, you could forget that anyone was there.

Fifi beamed. That's exactly how it had been! She was starting to feel a whole lot better about the TV Show. Perhaps she would be able to do it after all... And after their

trip to Waterworld the next day, she was sure

everything would be OK!

The Friendship Club agreed – Fifi was going

to be **brilliant!**

Waterworld!

The next morning, Hello Kitty was coming

down the stairs when the phone rang. She ran

to answer it. All that Hello Kitty could hear at

first were the sound of sniffs and sobs coming

from the other end. **Who** was there? It

was Fifi! And she was crying.

She explained to Hello

Kitty that she had done

another run-through of

her talk that morning in

front of her parents and

brother and sister, and it

hadn't gone very well at all.

Hello Kitty's heart sank. What could have

gone wrong? The practice run had gone

brilliantly only yesterday.

Fifi replied that it had started OK, but that

when she had started to talk about her friends,

for some reason she kept getting all their names

in a muddle. She started off by saying that Hello Kitty's dad travelled lots and that Dear Daniel had a sister called Mimmy, but *of course* it was the other way round! Hello Kitty groaned. Poor Fifi. Fifi said her parents had had to remind her what to say and then she'd had to start all over again.

When she had moved on to the birthdays' page her dad had made a movement like a camera rolling and it had made her feel nervous all over again. As she had started showing the pile of birthday cards and saying that they could be stuck into the scrapbook, she had been really clumsy and ended up knocking them on to the floor. Her little brother and sister had *rushed* forward to help pick them up but by then she had been all flustered.

She told Hello Kitty that she had ended up cutting the photos for the family moments' page too small and gluing them all in the book the wrong way up. When she

turned the scrapbook over, all of the people were missing their heads and upside down! Fifi wailed that she would **never** be able to do it well enough on the TV show. What if it went wrong when she was there?

Hello Kitty tried to reassure her. It had been just fine when she had done it yesterday – in fact, Fifi had been great! Hello Kitty was positive she would be fine again on the show.

It was probably just last minute nerves, but Fifi wasn't so sure. She didn't think she could go through with it after all.

Hello Kitty declared that Fifi **would** feel better later that day after she had taken her mind off it for a while, and they had the trip to Waterworld that morning to do just that. Fifi agreed, but she still sounded

tearful. Right now, she didn't want to go on the programme at all!

As Hello Kitty put down the phone she felt upset for her friend. If only there was something she could do to help.

Hopefully Waterworld would help distract Fifi from her worries.

Whoop!

Waterworld was full of the sound of laughter and happy shouting as Hello Kitty and her friends carried their towels out of the changing rooms and into the big swimming park. Hello Kitty was dressed in a **spotty** pink and white swimming costume with a matching pink swimming hat. Fifi was in a pale blue bikini with butterflies and Tammy was in a purple swimsuit with a big heart on the front. Dear Daniel was in his favourite bright red and

55

white stripy swimming shorts. To Hello Kitty's

relief, Waterworld did seem to be taking Fifi's

mind off the TV show. So far she hadn't said

anything more about it that morning. In fact,

she looked really quite relaxed and **happy**.

Maybe she was feeling OK now? Hello Kitty

definitely hoped so!

Hello Kitty looked around. Giant, brightly-coloured slides twisted and turned above their heads before plunging **down** into the clear water of the main swimming pool, which also had two big diving boards. There was a smaller pool for toddlers filled with blow-up toys, a pool for everyone to play in and another pool with lanes marked out for more serious swimmers.

Hello Kitty *and friends*

There was **even** a wave pool! Over the top of them all there was a big glass bubble; it was like being in a giant greenhouse. It was heated inside so it felt cosy and warm, even when you were just out of the water.

Hello Kitty suggested they go on the slides first.

Dear Daniel wanted to go on the diving
boards instead, so they decided to meet him
over by the fountain afterwards. It was
shaped like a **giant** white
mushroom and had water
spilling out of it.

Fifi rushed towards
the stairs to the slides,
followed by Tammy and
Hello Kitty. They made their
way up the staircase, and were
careful to hold on to the railings all the way up.
They were going to start on the green slide first
– the easiest one – and build themselves up to

the red, which was the hardest and twisted and turned all the way down to the water.

After they slid down giggling and **splashed** into the pool, they made their way over to the fountain. Hello Kitty pointed up to the diving boards. Dear Daniel was standing at the very top of one. He dived off smoothly and landed with a splash in the water!

He waved to them
as he swam over to
the giant fountain
and then they
all went to the
play pool. It
was filled with balls and floating toys, and had
basketball rings all around it.

The four friends split into teams and soon
they were throwing a ball between themselves,
taking it in turns to score goals.

Time was passing very quickly. Hello Kitty
looked at the **big** clock. They would just
have time for the wave pool before it was time

to go. Her mama was watching them from the glass viewing-platform and was pointing at her watch. Hello Kitty nodded and called to her friends. Quickly, they all ran over to the wave pool and dived in for their last **splashy** fun of the morning!

All too soon, play was at an end. Everyone had hot showers and got dry before meeting Mama White. She had got them all a hot chocolate to warm them up. *Yummy!*

As they sat by the side of the biggest pool sipping their hot chocolates, they chatted excitedly about finishing the friendship scrapbook that evening. They were going to put in a sports' page and a page of friendship sayings, and then it would all be done and ready for the show.

As Mama White drove them home to Fifi's house, they chatted happily. She dropped them at the gate and watched as they ran inside.

Hello Kitty waved goodbye to Mama and closed the door behind herself as Fifi ran up the stairs to get her scrapbook. But when Fifi came back down, she had a look of horror on her face.

It wasn't there! The friendship scrapbook had vanished! **Oh no!** Where could it have gone?

Everyone looked at each other. How could

the friendship scrapbook have gone missing?

Maybe Fifi's little brother or sister had taken

it for something. They ran into the kitchen to ask but Fifi's mum said that was *impossible*. Neither Fifi's brother or sister would have touched it; they knew how important it was. She gently suggested that perhaps it had got lost among all the painters' things. They had laid out even more dust sheets that morning, but they would be moving them later so it would be easier to see. There was no need to panic just yet.

The Friendship Club agreed. They were sure that Fifi's mother was right and to take their minds off it, she announced that they could

watch a movie together. **Hooray!** They all settled down on beanbags to choose a movie with Fifi snuggled in the middle, relaxed and happy. Brilliant!

A Surprise Discovery

When Hello Kitty knocked on Fifi's door

the next day, Fifi opened it herself. She looked

very happy, so Hello Kitty thought that it could

only mean one thing – that she had found the

scrapbook! But Fifi told her it was still missing.

She led Hello Kitty inside, putting in that Dear

Daniel and Tammy were just on their way.

Hello Kitty was **surprised** that Fifi

wasn't more anxious, but perhaps the fact that

everyone was going to be helping her to search

for it that morning was making her feel more at

ease. She suggested they start looking for it but

Fifi thought they could have a game of hide and

seek while they waited for the others instead
— it would be fun! Hello Kitty was even more
surprised! She knew that if it had been her,
she would have wanted to get looking for the
scrapbook straightaway. Still, if Fifi wanted to
play hide-and-seek, then hide-and-seek it was.
Fifi asked Hello Kitty to count to ten while she
went to hide. She asked Hello Kitty not to hide
in her bedroom as it was a complete mess and
she needed to put stuff away.

Hello Kitty nodded and Fifi ran off to hide.

One.... *Two*... *Three*... Hello Kitty
counted under her breath. ...*Nine*....
Ten... Coming, ready or not!

Hello Kitty started by looking under the stairs; it was always Fifi's favourite hiding place. But for once, she wasn't there. *Hmmm...* Hello Kitty made her way into the playroom, and then she laughed.

She had seen the curtains twitching and knew exactly where Fifi was! But she decided to make Fifi wait and pretended to look behind the door and under the table before she pounced.

Boo! Fifi jumped high in the air and the two girls exploded into fits of laughter. Now, it was Hello Kitty's turn to hide.

Fifi quickly started counting to ten as Hello Kitty hurried out of the room and up the stairs. She could still hear Fifi counting down below. Now she was at

eight... Nine...

Hello Kitty tiptoed across the landing as fast as she could. But where to hide? The bathroom? The study? Then suddenly she heard Fifi call out 'Ten'... Now she was coming up the stairs! There wasn't time! Hello Kitty dived through the nearest door, which happened to be to Fifi's bedroom.

Hello Kitty looked around her. Of course she wasn't meant to be in there, but now that she saw it she wasn't sure why. It didn't look messy *at all!* Hello Kitty was about to back out when she saw something poking out from under the bed. It had a purple corner with little silver stars on it. Wasn't that the friendship scrapbook?

Hello Kitty reached

down and pulled it out. She gasped. **It was!** But

what was it doing under Fifi's bed? Wasn't that

where Fifi had said she put all her secret stuff?

Hello Kitty thought hard. The book being

under the bed could only mean one thing – Fifi

must have hidden it there! **But why?**

It didn't make sense.

Why would she wreck her own chances of being on the TV show?

At that moment, Fifi **pushed** back the door. Hello Kitty was still holding the book in her hands.

Oh. The two girls looked at each other. Hello Kitty went pink and started to say how sorry

she was — she knew that she wasn't meant to be in Fifi's bedroom. But then Fifi blushed bright red and looked very guilty!

Hello Kitty held the book up. **Whatever** was going on?

Fifi gulped. She looked at the floor and admitted that she had hidden the scrapbook herself. She had been going to own up and tell everyone what she had done after the TV show had been filmed.

After the TV show? Hello Kitty was shocked.

But then... that would mean that Fifi wouldn't

have been able to go on it!

Fifi nodded slowly. That had been the plan.

Hello Kitty didn't understand. She had

thought that Fifi was feeling all right about

the TV show after their phone call, but Fifi

whispered that she wasn't feeling all right at all. She felt scared stiff. She had been fine doing her presenting speech when her friends were there, but when they weren't and it had been in front of her parents, all of a sudden she had thought about what it would be like presenting to strangers and had felt so nervous she messed it all up! She didn't think she could do it after all, so she had hidden the scrapbook so she wouldn't have to go on the show. She hung her head. Was Hello Kitty cross with her, she asked quietly?

Hello Kitty smiled. Of course not! She rushed over and gave Fifi a big hug. She

just wanted to make it better. Hello Kitty knew

that Fifi could do the presenting. She just wished

that Fifi knew that too...

Hello Kitty thought hard. An idea started

to form in her head – one of her *special,*

super, Hello Kitty ideas! What if the

Friendship Club came with Fifi to the TV show? Would that help? She had been just fine doing her presenting in front of the Friendship Club. Maybe if they were all there to support her in the audience it would give Fifi the confidence she needed.

Fifi nodded eagerly. She was **sure** it would. But would it be possible? Hello Kitty nodded. They would have to ask Fifi's mum, but maybe there would be some space in the studio

audience for the Friendship Club. Fifi really

hoped there would be! But then a troubled look

crossed her face. **What** would the others

say when they found out about her hiding the

scrapbook? What if they were cross with her?

Hello Kitty smiled, and told Fifi not to worry

– it could be their special secret. No one else

needed to know.

At that very moment, there was a knock on the door and Tammy and Dear Daniel rushed in. They were **SOOO** excited when they saw the scrapbook and questions flooded the room as they asked where Fifi had found the scrapbook! Hello Kitty looked across at Fifi and grinned. She announced that it had been under

something... a pile of decorator's pots! It was

half true, after all.

After Fifi and Hello Kitty told the others

about Hello Kitty's idea, the Friendship Club

didn't dwell on the details for too long. What

was important was that they

had found the scrapbook,

and that Fifi would still

be able to be

a presenter!

Fifi *ran* downstairs

to talk to her mum, who

made a phone call to the TV

company and then let the Friendship Club know

the good news – they could all go and watch

Fifi's presentation, as long as their parents

agreed – how super was that! And there was

even just enough time for another run-through

and, this time, Fifi was word perfect! All that

was left was for them to go home and get some

sleep ahead of the big day!

Lights, Camera, Action!

Hello Kitty looked across to where Fifi stood to the left of the stage. She was in darkness, as the main action was still taking place in the centre where the TV presenter was talking to the studio audience. It was a big room with

lots of rows of seats, and the ceiling overhead was filled with layers and layers of lights, of all shapes and sizes.

Right in front of Fifi there was a large table, laid out with her all her materials and props and of course, the all-important friendship scrapbook! People with TV cameras were wheeling their cameras around **everywhere**, and lights were flashing as they did the last sound and lighting checks. Hello Kitty, Fifi and Dear Daniel were right in the front row, where Fifi could see them easily from where she stood. Finally, it was time to begin the show!

The presenter introduced Fifi to the audience, and then the lights and cameras flashed to Fifi's table.

Fifi looked out nervously for a moment but then she spotted her friends in the row right in front. They all gave her big *grins*, and Hello Kitty gave her a thumbs-up. Fifi took a deep breath and smiled.

The cameras rolled, the clapperboard clicked down and Fifi started her presentation to the audience. She began by introducing the friendship scrapbook, and she didn't mess up **at all!** She went on, talking about her family and friends and their birthdays, showing all the things that could go into making a scrapbook, and how to decorate the different pages. She

Hello Kitty *and friends*

explained how to cut things out and stick them in and made suggestions for things to put on each of the pages.

She kept going, looking more confident all the time, and talked about how to put together

special family moments

with photos and highlight

them with a family tree,

before going on to the

other pages. Finally, she finished on the page

about friendship sayings. When she started to

talk about the friendship sayings, she looked

across at her

friends and

smiled as

she ran through

the different

ones they had

come up with

Good Friends come in all shapes and sizes

in the Friendship Club. Like good friends always being there when you needed them, and coming in all shapes and sizes. She had one more to add, she said, and her eyes **twinkled** as she declared that it would have to wait until the cameras finished rolling, as she needed to tell it to the

Good friends are always there when you need them most!

Friendship Club before she could share it on TV! Everyone laughed and clapped.

As the filming finished and the audience continued to applaud, the director came on and announced to everyone how *pleased* he was that Fifi had been able to come and turn her hand to presenting. He thought she had done a great job. In fact he had better watch out or she would be taking over the show! They all giggled.

Fifi blushed, and said **loudly** that she wouldn't even be on the show if it wasn't for her friends. She explained how very nervous she had been, but that her friends had been there for her and persuaded her to do it. Because...

Good friends are always there to understand.

She and Hello Kitty shared a secret smile.

In fact, she announced, she had decided that

she was going to add that as the special

new Friendship Club saying! Everyone in

the audience clapped and cheered, and the

Friendship Club all nodded and beamed at each

other. They knew they would always be there

to understand and support each other, and to

be the best of friends – forever and ever!

The end

Turn over the page for activities and
fun things that you can do with your
friends – just like Hello Kitty!

Fantastic Friendship Scrapbook!

Having friends is the best fun ever, and sometimes it's nice to show them you care. A great way to do this is by making a friendship scrapbook, just like Fifi! Just follow these simple instructions and get crafty!

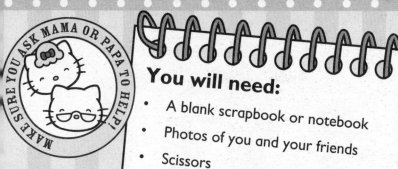

MAKE SURE YOU ASK MAMA OR PAPA TO HELP!

You will need:

- A blank scrapbook or notebook
- Photos of you and your friends
- Scissors
- Glue
- Old magazines to cut up
- Coloured pens and pencils
- Craft supplies to decorate with, like glitter, stickers, ribbons and sequins!

And lots of imagination!

Pick your pages!

The first thing you will need to do is decide
how many pages you have to fill up,
and what you want to put on them.
If you have lots of friends you will need more space for
each type of page too – if you have four friends you can
fit all their birthdays on two pages, but if you have ten
friends you might want to use four... Use the ideas on
these pages, or come up with some more of your own!

Birthday Buddies

Put photos of your friends,
with their birth dates
underneath. Now you'll
never forget!

Travel Time!

You can stick pictures from
magazines of places you
would all like to go, or even
souvenirs of places you've
already been.

Magical memories

This section is all about the great times you've had with your friends. You can put in photos or souvenirs, or write stories about all the fun times you've had!

Super-stylish!

All your friends have their own style, and so do you! Use these pages to show off your fashion sense – you can use photos, pictures from magazines, or even design your ultimate outfit...

Sports pals

Who loves sports? Hello Kitty and her friends sure do! Use these pages to show which sports you and your friends like to do, what you're good at, and which teams you love!

GLUE

What's in a Name?

Finally, you need to decide on what you want to call your scrapbook, and how you want the cover to look! Hello Kitty's scrapbook is called The Friendship Club Family, and it has a picture of them in a big glittery heart on the front! What will you call yours? Here are some friendship words to get you started...

- *Friends*
- *Pals*
- *Amigos*
- *Buddies*
- *Mates*

You're on TV

Have you ever dreamed of being on TV just like Fifi? Well now you can!

MAKE SURE YOU ASK MAMA OR PAPA TO HELP!

You will need:

A big cardboard box

Scissors

Glue

A marker pen

Clear cling film / sandwich wrap

Bottle tops

What to do

1. Turn the box upside down, so the open top is on the ground. Ask a grown-up to help you draw a big square on the front side of the box, and cut it out. This will be your screen!

2. Draw a big border around the hole, and decorate around it by gluing on the bottle tops like TV knobs. You can label them with things like CHANNEL or VOLUME if you like...

3. Cover the cut-out hole with cling film, from the inside. You will need to stick it to the inside of the box, just around the edges of the big hole, so that from the outside it just looks like a clear screen!

4. Climb inside, and you're on TV! Now you decide what people will watch – do you want to tell them the news, or make them laugh? Just don't forget to shout if they turn up the volume knob!

Turn the page for a sneak peek at

Hello Kitty

and friends'

next adventure...

The Big Race

Hello Kitty put her books away and started to draw a doodle as the rest of the class finished packing up. She sketched a pretty flower and then turned it into a fluffy pom-pom. She was so busy drawing and colouring in that she nearly didn't hear their class teacher, Miss Davey, tell them she had an important announcement to make. Whoops!

Hello Kitty put her pencil down and glanced quickly across the table. Her friends Fifi, Tammy and Dear Daniel were all looking expectantly at Miss Davey. Hello Kitty smiled – they were her best friends. Such great friends in fact that they had started a club, and together the four of them made up the Friendship Club! They met up all the time to do loads of fun things like crafting and baking and having fashion makeovers.

Miss Davey waited until she had the whole class's attention and everyone was completely silent before she started to speak. She began by telling them all that there were only three days left till half-term holidays, but Hello Kitty and the class already knew that, of course! They all knew what they were going to do in the holidays. Dear Daniel was going away travelling with his dad, but the rest of the Friendship Club were spending the break at home. They had already made plans for lots of fun things to do together – like sleepovers, makeovers, and trips out – and Hello Kitty couldn't wait! Just then, Miss Davey made her big announcement. The teachers had decided that there was going to be a cross-country race on Friday to finish off the term with a bang, followed by a family picnic! How SUPER was that! She asked people to put their hands up if they wanted to enter the race...

Find out what happens next in...

Out now!

Hello Kitty
and friends

The Big Race
· A HELLO KITTY ADVENTURE ·

Hello Kitty
and friends

The TV Star
· A HELLO KITTY ADVENTURE ·

The Friendship Club

The School Trip

The Summer Fair

The Pop Princess

The Wedding Day

The Beach Holiday

The Treasure Hunt

The Talent Show

The Christmas Present
TWO SPECIAL CHRISTMAS STORIES